W9-BTT-701

SPINE SHIVERS

St. Mark's Anglican School Library
PO Box 231 Hillarys 6025
PH: (08) 9403 1300

SPINE SHIVERS BOOKS ARE PUBLISHED BY STONE ARCH BOOKS
A CAPSTONE IMPRINT
1710 ROE CREST DRIVE
NORTH MANKATO, MINNESOTA 56003
WWW.CAPSTONEPUB.COM

© 2016 STONE ARCH BOOKS

ALL RIGHTS RESERVED. NO PART OF THIS PUBLICATION MAY BE REPRODUCED IN WHOLE OR IN
PART, OR STORED IN A RETRIEVAL SYSTEM, OR TRANSMITTED IN ANY FORM OR BY ANY MEANS,
ELECTRONIC, MECHANICAL, PHOTOCOPYING, RECORDING, OR OTHERWISE, WITHOUT WRITTEN
PERMISSION OF THE PUBLISHER.

LIBRARY OF CONGRESS CATALOGING-IN-PUBLICATION

DARKE, J. A., AUTHOR.
  THE SCREAMING BRIDGE / BY J. A. DARKE ; TEXT BY BRANDON TERRELL ; COVER
ILLUSTRATION BY NELSON EVERGREEN.
    PAGES CM. -- (SPINE SHIVERS)

  SUMMARY: WHEN SHE HEARS THE STORY ABOUT THE SCREAMING BRIDGE, WHERE A BUSLOAD
OF ORPHANS WERE KILLED FIFTY YEARS BEFORE, SIXTEEN-YEAR-OLD EMMA DONOVAN AND HER
FRIENDS DECIDE TO INVESTIGATE THE ABANDONED ORPHANAGE AND THE BRIDGE—AND THAT IS
THE BEGINNING OF A TERRIFYING NIGHT FOR EMMA.

  ISBN 978-1-4965-0219-3 (LIBRARY BINDING) -- ISBN 978-1-4965-0376-3 (PBK.) -- ISBN
978-1-4965-2355-6 (EBOOK PDF)

1. HAUNTED PLACES--JUVENILE FICTION. 2. BRIDGES--JUVENILE FICTION. 3. ORPHANAGES--
JUVENILE FICTION. 4. GHOST STORIES. 5. HORROR TALES. [1. HAUNTED PLACES--FICTION. 2.
BRIDGES--FICTION. 3. ORPHANAGES--FICTION. 4. GHOSTS--FICTION. 5. HORROR STORIES.] I.
TERRELL, BRANDON, 1978- AUTHOR. II. EVERGREEN, NELSON, 1971- ILLUSTRATOR. III. TITLE.

PZ7.1.D33SC 2016
813.6--DC23
[FIC]

                              2014043751

DESIGNER: HILARY WACHOLZ

PRINTED IN CHINA BY NORDICA.
0415/CA21500559
032015   008841NORDF15

THE SCREAMING BRIDGE

BY J. A. DARKE

TEXT BY BRANDON TERRELL

ILLUSTRATED BY NELSON EVERGREEN

STONE ARCH BOOKS
a capstone imprint

TABLE OF CONTENTS

CHAPTER 1

"*Ahhhh!*" Lucy O'Connell let out a blood-curdling scream and waved her arms in front of her as she backed into a corner of her bedroom. "Get it away from me! Eww! *Ewww!*"

Her best friend, Emma Donovan, laughed and hopped up from the bed, where she'd been sitting while she scrolled through pictures on her phone. "Chill out, Lucy," she said. "It's just a moth."

"I don't care what it is! It dive-bombed my face!" Lucy said, shuddering.

Emma snorted back laughter. She watched as the winged insect fluttered around Lucy's bedroom, finally landing on the domed ceiling light. Its brown and black speckled wings twitched and then closed.

Emma dragged a wooden chair from the desk, climbed onto it, and reached up to the light. Slowly, calmly, she cupped her hands around the moth. Then she said, "Open the window, Luce."

Lucy, nose still wrinkled in disgust, dashed to the window and threw it open. A cool wind snaked inside and wrapped itself around Emma, making her shiver.

Emma could feel the moth's wings tickle her palms as she reached her cupped hands out the window. She released the moth, watching it fly up into the darkening October sky until it disappeared. Then she closed the window again. "There," she said. "It's gone. Better?"

"Much. Thanks," Lucy said, letting out a deep breath.

"No prob."

Though no sixteen-year-old liked to admit it, most still held on to their childhood fears. Some were afraid of the dark, some of heights, and some — as in Lucy's case, apparently — of harmless insects searching for light and warmth.

Not Emma, though. Emma didn't get scared. Emma had always been fearless. She'd always been the first to catch a snake or a frog or a millipede. The first to climb to the top of the jungle gym in elementary school, balancing atop it as easily as an Olympic gymnast.

One Halloween, when Emma was nine years old, her older brother Peter had tried to pull a prank on her. He'd dressed up as a scarecrow and sat in a plastic chair on the front porch of their house, his arms and legs and head dangling limp, pretending to be nothing more than flannel and overalls and a mask stuffed with straw. When Emma had returned home from trick-or-treating, a pillowcase full of candy slung triumphantly over one shoulder, Peter had leaped from his chair right in front of her and snarled in his best undead scarecrow voice, "Boo!"

Emma didn't jump. She didn't scream or cry or drop her trove of goodies and run away in fear like Peter had hoped she would. Instead, Emma's reaction had been to punch the scarecrow right in its face. She'd given Peter a black eye that his friends would not let him live down for the rest of the school year.

Lucy, shaking off her fear of moths, went back to rummaging in her closet. "The guys will be here any minute," she said. "Unless they're already here. Can you check?"

Emma glanced out the window at the tree-lined street outside Lucy's house. Lamps were sparking to life, leaving pools of light and long shadows of swaying tree branches in the dusk. The street was empty.

"Nope," she answered. "Not yet."

"Good." Lucy plucked her fifth outfit in as many minutes out of the closet and changed into it. This one was a dark purple sweater with skinny jeans.

"So who's this guy Connor is bringing with him tonight?" Emma asked. Connor was Lucy's boyfriend.

"His name is Daniel," Lucy explained. "He's one of Connor's lacrosse buddies from Rush Valley. I've only met him once, at a party. Dark eyes. Dark hair. Dimples. Mmmm. He's cute. You'll like him." Lucy twirled in a circle. "Do you think I'll be warm enough in this?"

"Yeah, you'll be fine."

"I don't know," Lucy said as she began to sort through her closet again. Emma rolled her eyes and dropped back onto Lucy's bed. Unlike Emma, who prided herself on being dependable, Lucy changed her mind about as often as a hummingbird changes its flying pattern. Oddly enough, though, that was one of the things Emma loved about her friend. The two besties were so different that, to someone who didn't know them, they looked like they would fit together like a round hole and a square peg.

Lucy stopped searching for a new outfit and turned to face her friend. She placed her hands on her hips and said, with a very serious expression, "Emma, I say this with nothing but love, but are you sure you want to go on a double date dressed like you're about to walk to the gas station to buy a slushie and a frozen burrito?"

"Listen," Emma said, grabbing a square, pink pillow and chucking it at Lucy. "I dressed for comfort tonight." She wore a simple black hooded sweatshirt, a pair of her favorite jeans, and bright red sneakers. "Dimples or not, I don't care about impressing this Daniel dude."

"Well, you just might change your mind once you see him," Lucy said.

Emma rolled her eyes and checked the time on her phone. It was almost seven o'clock. "If they don't get here soon, we're not gonna make the movie," she said.

The real reason Emma was excited for her blind date with Connor's friend wasn't the boy. It was their destination for the evening. They were going to the Rialto Theatre, one of the only remaining single-screen movie theaters in the state. The Rialto was hosting a special premiere of *Invasion from Planet X: Part 6*, the newest installment in Emma's all-time favorite movie series. The theater would be packed with horror fans. Many would be dressed as Zom-borg, the half-undead, half-robotic main villain in the series. Emma had been waiting for this premiere event since the theater had announced it a few months before. She'd avoided all of the movie spoilers and set photos posted online, an act that had required more self-control than she'd ever imagined. But she'd done it.

"Dimples isn't going to talk through the whole movie, is he?" Emma asked, truly concerned.

Lucy shrugged. "I don't know how he feels about movie etiquette, Em."

"If he does, so help me, he's getting an elbow to the ribs."

"I would expect nothing less from you," Lucy said. She smiled at her friend before turning back to the mirrored closet door.

"Maybe I should bring a roll of duct tape in case he feels like chatting," Emma said.

"Emma, relax," Lucy said. "You'll get to see your movie."

Honk! Honk!

Lucy gasped. "They're here! Oh no, this outfit is terrible. I have to change!" She quickly shed her purple sweater and put on a nearly identical purple and white striped wool sweater. Emma looked out the window. Sure enough, a black car with a dented front bumper was now parked in front of Lucy's house, its headlights glaring. The stereo volume was so loud, Emma could hear and practically feel the bass from Lucy's bedroom.

Connor was climbing out of the car. When he saw Emma looking out the window, he waved up at her. She waved back.

"Come on, let's go," Lucy said as she grabbed Emma's arm and pulled her out the bedroom door.

They passed Lucy's parents in the living room. Her dad was sitting in a well-loved recliner watching one of the twenty-four-hour news channels, the television remote resting on his ample stomach. Lucy's mother sat sipping tea and reading a book whose crinkling dust jacket showed that she had checked it out from the library. Before the two girls were able to escape the house, Lucy's dad stopped them by loudly clearing his throat.

"*Ahem!* Use your heads tonight, girls," he said. "You both have phones. I expect you to use them if you need to. Am I clear?"

"Crystal," Lucy answered.

"Your curfew is midnight," he said. "No later. Got it?"

"Yes, Daddy."

"And tell that boyfriend of yours to turn his stereo down before someone's ears start bleeding," he said. "I can hear it from here."

Lucy rolled her eyes.

"Have fun at the movie, girls," Lucy's mom added with a smile. Then she made a shooing gesture.

"Bye!" Lucy sang, still holding tight to Emma's arm as the two breezed out the front door.

The moon outside was not quite full, but close. Soon it would be dark, and the cloudless sky would be brimming with stars. There was a bite in the air that Emma loved. Fall was her favorite time of year. She loved the way trees blazed bright colors in the sun. Hot apple cider and pumpkins. Halloween. Soon winter would arrive, blanketing the town in snow. Emma shoved her hands into the giant pouch in the front of her sweatshirt for warmth.

"There they are! Hello, ladies!" Connor's wide smile filled his square-jawed face. He was tall and muscular and blond, the kind of guy who looked like he could be the captain of any and all high school sports teams. While Connor was, in fact, the captain of the lacrosse team at their high school, he never flaunted it. And he always wore his dad's olive green military jacket, never a sports jacket.

Emma had once watched Lucy's boyfriend take apart the engine block of his dad's Mustang with zero effort, yet he had trouble remembering who fought who in the Spanish-American War. He was often loud and obnoxious, but he treated Lucy like a queen. For that, he had Emma's respect.

Lucy ran up to Connor. He whisked her off the ground and into his arms. She laughed and threw her head back.

Ugh. They make me wanna puke, Emma thought.

Instead of throwing up her dinner, though, she opened one of the car's back doors and climbed in. It stank of body spray inside, but at least the guy sitting in the passenger's seat had been kind enough to turn the stereo volume down as she settled in behind him.

Daniel turned around to face her. He had

dark hair that swooped across his forehead, piercing gray eyes, and, yeah, dimples.

Lucy was right about the dimples, Emma thought.

"Hi," he said, reaching back to shake her hand. "I'm Daniel."

"Emma." His hand was cold and clammy, but she shook it anyway.

"Should be a fun night," Daniel said. "Connor said you're really excited to see this movie."

Emma nodded. "Connor spoke truth."

"Cool."

"Have you seen any of the other films in the series?" Emma asked.

"Uh, no. Sorry. Still, it . . . uh . . . it looks good," Daniel said.

It's official. Awkward conversation while stuck alone together in a car is not the ideal way to meet someone, Emma decided.

Thankfully, the door beside her opened and Lucy leaped inside. She pressed in next to Emma. "Hi, Daniel," she said in her best singsong voice.

"Hey, Lucy," Daniel said.

Lucy nudged Emma with an elbow and raised her eyebrows in a clear *So, what do you think?* gesture.

Emma shrugged her shoulders, but she gave Lucy a tiny smile.

Lucy pointed to one of her cheeks and mouthed, *Dimples? Right?*

Emma nudged her with a shoulder. *Knock it off,* she mouthed back.

Connor dropped in behind the wheel and cranked the volume of the radio back up to ear-splitting levels. "All right!" he shouted. "Who's ready to see a scary movie?"

Finally, Emma thought.

The car jerked forward, and they took off down the road.

CHAPTER 2

Connor was a terrible driver. He was often distracted, either by Lucy giggling and smiling at him in the rearview mirror or by trying to find the perfect song to play on the radio. He rolled down his window and hung an arm out, hitting the side of his car to the beat of the music. Emma was thankful for the seat belt buckled tightly across her lap.

Sterling was a small town. It had only a few stoplights and a shopping district that was three blocks long. If you wanted to hit the chain stores, you had to drive about twenty minutes to Peyton or Rush Valley.

Emma checked her watch. The movie would be starting any minute now.

"What's the matter?" Lucy asked with a sly smile. "Got a hot date? Oh wait . . ." She leaned in and whispered, "You're already on one." Then she laughed hysterically.

Emma leaned her forehead against the cool glass of the window. There was no sense in talking to Lucy. With the radio volume so loud, she'd have to scream directly into her friend's ear to be heard. Plus, Lucy had her arms wrapped around the seat in front of her and across Connor's chest.

Emma watched as houses zipped past the window. The Rialto Theatre was located on the west edge of town, past the high school and a string of chain restaurants and small clothing shops.

Finally, they approached the corner where the Rialto had been showing movies for nearly a century. Emma saw the blinking lights beaming from the theater's entrance.

As Connor pulled into a parking lot across the street from the theater, Emma spotted a line of people outside the theater. She feared that by the time they got to the ticket booth, the premiere would be sold out.

Emma unbuckled her seat belt and leaped out the moment Connor parked the car.

"Whoa! Someone's anxious," Connor said. Emma barely heard him. She was already crossing the street to get a place in line. Daniel did his best to keep up with her, while Lucy and Connor walked to the theater entrance at a much slower pace.

Thankfully, when Emma and her friends reached the ticket window, the show was not sold out. Inside, the theater's lobby was two stories tall, with red velvet walls and carpeting and a huge glass chandelier that reflected glints of light in every direction. Posters from classic movies hung along the walls. There was an ancient machine popping delicious, buttery-smelling popcorn.

The lobby was packed with people. Emma had been right about the costumes. A number of people walked through the crowd or stood in line at the concession stand dressed as their favorite horror movie characters. There was a fair share of Zomborgs among them. She saw one chowing down on a large tub of popcorn, fumbling to get a handful into his mouth. Another slurped from a massive cup of soda, while a third enjoyed some candy.

"You guys save us some seats," Connor said. "We'll get the snacks."

Emma had no problem with that. While Connor and Lucy stood in line for snacks, she led Daniel into the theater. She knew exactly where they should sit for the best viewing experience. Unfortunately, those seats were already taken. But she spied four seats two rows back that were still available.

"There!" Emma said, pointing to the seats.

Emma hurried up the aisle steps to the seats. She made sure Daniel draped his coat over the other two seats before someone else came by and snatched them. Soon the lights dimmed, and the previews began playing. Emma saw her friends enter, their arms filled with soda cups and popcorn buckets. Connor and Lucy searched the darkness. Emma waved. When Lucy spotted her, she stumbled over with Connor following. They plopped down in the two empty seats, Lucy next to Emma and Connor beside her.

"Will you make sure I don't get too scared?" Lucy playfully asked her boyfriend.

"Absolutely," he answered.

"Barf," Emma said, taking one of the popcorn tubs for her and Daniel. Soon the trailers ended, and with a mighty cheer from the crowd, the movie began.

For the next two hours, from the moment the movie's title appeared in blood-red type on the screen until the supposedly dead Zom-borg made one more surprising attack, Emma was enthralled. Lucy screamed and leaped at every scare, making the people sitting around them laugh nervously.

At one point during the movie, Emma glanced at Daniel. He seemed to be enjoying it as much as she was, and he wasn't talking over the movie, which Emma appreciated.

When the last of the credits flickered across the giant screen, many of the moviegoers stood up to walk out of the theater, talking excitedly about what they'd just seen.

"Man," Connor said as their group headed toward the lobby, "that movie was awesome."

"Yeah, it was way scarier than I thought it would be," Lucy added, even though she'd spent much of the movie shielding her eyes.

"Luce, it was a horror movie," Connor said. "How did you not think it would be scary?"

"What did you think of the movie, Emma?" Daniel asked.

Emma shrugged. "It wasn't the best in the series, but it was still good. Kind of like pizza. Even when it's bad, it's still good."

"Speaking of pizza, you guys wanna get a bite to eat?" Connor asked. "I'm super hungry. We could hit Al's for some grub."

"I don't know," Emma said. "Our curfew is creeping up on us. We should probably get home. Right, Luce?"

Lucy looked shocked at the thought, which, in hindsight, Emma should've realized would be her reaction. "Em, you know my parents aren't sitting up waiting for us."

She had a point. Emma was near certain that Lucy's parents were already in bed, fast asleep, her father snoring away and her mother resting peacefully thanks to the giant pink earplugs she wore every night.

"All right, fine," she said. "I could eat."

CHAPTER 3

Albert's Diner was an all-night restaurant that was located across the street from the Rialto Theatre. It had been a Sterling staple for decades. In fact, the old place still had the same wobbly Formica tables and torn plastic booths it had back when it had first opened in the 1950s. A long counter ran through the center of the diner. The fluorescent lighting gave the place a drab appearance.

At this time of night, it wasn't terribly crowded. Emma recognized a few kids who went to their school sitting in a corner booth. There were also a few tables filled with fellow moviegoers who'd had the same idea as them, including a guy dressed like Zom-borg eating a slice of apple pie. A few older patrons were perched at the counter, sipping from white ceramic coffee mugs.

The quartet found a booth near the diner's plate-glass window that looked out onto the parking lot where Connor had parked before the movie. Streetlights swarming with insects cast the lot in a pale greenish glow. Connor and Lucy crowded into one side of the booth, while Emma and Daniel sat on the other.

As he slid into the booth, Daniel accidentally brushed Emma's arm. "Oh," he said, "sorry, Emma."

"That's okay," Emma said. Daniel was very polite, and he seemed like a really nice guy. But unfortunately for Dimples, Emma didn't find him very interesting.

Their waitress, an older lady whose gray hair was twisted up in a bun and held in place by a ballpoint pen, came over and slapped down a stack of menus. The group ordered sodas, which she quickly brought over. They arrived in tall red plastic cups. Emma took a long swig. She was starting to get sleepy and hoped the boost of caffeine would help.

After the waitress had taken their food order and walked away with the menus tucked under her arm, Connor's lips curled into a sly smile. "Man, I still can't believe that movie," he said. "When the thing burst out of the guy's chest . . ." He whistled in appreciation.

Emma nodded. "Yeah, that was pretty surprising," she said. "You could tell it was all computer effects, though. It didn't look very real."

"You *wanted* it to look real?" Lucy asked, incredulous. "Disgusting. Only you, Em."

"Yes. I mean, no," Emma said. "It's just . . . well, movies used to be a lot scarier when they used practical effects and didn't rely on computers all the time. The first *Invasion from Planet X* was all latex masks and corn syrup blood."

"Wait, they make fake blood out of corn syrup?" Connor asked.

"Sometimes," Emma replied. "They mix it with red food coloring."

"Sounds delicious," said Connor.

"Ew." Lucy wrinkled her nose in disgust.

The group sat in silence for a moment. Lucy began scrolling through her phone while Connor tried to read the screen over her shoulder. Emma watched as Daniel poured salt into a pile on the table and tried to balance the shaker at an angle on it. Then her gaze drifted out the window.

Finally, Daniel cleared his throat and quietly asked, "So . . . do you guys want to hear something *really* scary? Something that, like, actually happened?"

"Are you kidding?" Connor said without hesitation. "Of course."

"Nope," Lucy said.

Emma was intrigued. "Sure," she said, turning in the booth to face Daniel.

Daniel leaned forward. "Have any of you heard the story of the screaming bridge on old County Road Sixty-One?"

It was the first thing Dimples had said that interested Emma. "Wait, what's a screaming bridge?" she asked as she took another sip of soda.

"A haunted bridge," Daniel explained. "This one's between Sterling and Rush Valley, in the middle of nowhere. They shut it down back when they built the new highway, before we were even born."

"A haunted bridge?" Lucy asked. She shook her head. "No thank you. I don't want to hear about it. I'm already going to have nightmares because of that stupid movie we just saw."

Despite her best friend's objections, Emma was intrigued. She needed to know more. "Please don't tell me you read about it on one of those ridiculous Facebook links. 'This bridge is haunted, and you'll never guess why. Click here to find out!'"

Daniel chuckled. "No, I swear I didn't," he said.

"So what's the legend then?" she asked.

"Okay, apparently they have these bridges all over the country, and they're supposed to be haunted," Daniel said. "They're called 'screaming bridges' or 'cry-baby bridges.'"

"Already not a fan," Lucy interrupted.

Daniel said, "You know what. It's okay. I don't want to upset Lucy."

"Come on," Connor pleaded. "She's a big girl. She can handle it. Right, Luce?"

Lucy just glared at him.

Connor ignored her silent anger. "Keep talking, dude."

Daniel began again, hesitant this time. "Anyway . . . um, the bridge on old Sixty-One, the one that crosses over Sterling River, is supposedly a screaming bridge."

"What makes it a screaming bridge?" Emma asked.

"Well, I guess the spirits attached to these bridges either fell, jumped, or were thrown over the bridge. If you stop your car in the middle of the bridge, you can hear them screaming."

"You can hear the ghosts screaming?" Emma asked.

"Yeah."

"That's *horrible*," Lucy said.

"My great-grandpa Vernon told me about it last summer," Daniel explained. "He used to live out past the Judson farm, near the Washburn Orphanage. He was a milkman, and he delivered there."

"Wait, there's an orphanage in Rush Valley?" Connor asked.

"Used to be," Daniel said. He took a swig of his beverage. "It's been closed for years. Just a busted-up old building now."

"Have you been out there?" Connor asked.

"Yeah," said Daniel. "It's one of those places now that kids dare one another to visit at night. When I was about twelve, I overheard my brother and his buddies talking about the Washburn place, betting each other a hundred bucks on who could spend the night there."

"Did they?" Connor asked.

Daniel shook his head. "Not that I know about, anyway," he said. "I biked out there, though, later that afternoon, down a couple of gravel roads and over the bridge — which

I didn't know was haunted — until I got to the turn-off for the orphanage."

"What was it like?" Lucy asked, leaning closer.

"It was creepy," Daniel said. "Even in the middle of a sunny afternoon. Like . . . I don't know . . . like it was sucking up the light all around it. I didn't even make it to the front door. I turned around and pedaled home. Haven't been back since."

"Here ya are, kiddos." The waitress had appeared from nowhere, balancing a tray of food in one hand. She slid a basket with a cheeseburger perched atop a mass of French fries in front of Connor. Daniel had the same. Emma had chosen a simple hamburger — she hated all the extra garbage that came with them, everything but ketchup — while Lucy had ordered only a side order of onion rings.

"Anything else I can get ya?" the waitress asked.

All four shook their heads.

Emma slathered her burger in ketchup and added a pool in the basket to dip her fries in.

Connor took an enormous bite of his burger and said, while chewing, "So what'd your milkman great-grandpa say about this bridge? Why's it haunted?"

"I guess there was an accident with a bus coming from the Washburn Orphanage," Daniel said. "I'll tell you the story my great-grandpa told me . . ."

CHAPTER 4

It's hot, the kind of sweltering heat that takes your breath right out of your lungs and doesn't give it back. The year is 1953. The town of Sterling, which was once nothing more than a few brick buildings strung along one main street, is growing.

A man named Albert Reynolds — known to everyone in town as Uncle Albert — has just opened a diner, quite appropriately named Albert's Diner. It is booming with business, especially with high school kids who've spent their allowance to see a matinee over at the fancy Rialto Theatre. There are many new houses being constructed, and it's clear that the population of Sterling is changing. It's no longer just farm families living off the land.

Vernon Blake spends each day of the week delivering milk to the residents of his hometown, Sterling, the nearby Rush Valley, and every spot in between. And on this hot day, after making his Sterling deliveries and stopping at Al's for a pastrami sandwich and a cream soda, Vernon drives along County Road Sixty-One toward Rush Valley. There's one last stop to make today, the red brick building known as the Washburn Orphanage.

As he turns onto the drive and pulls up beside the orphanage's main doors, he spots a white and yellow school bus. Children of all ages — some as young as four, others battling the awkward pre-teen years — stand outside. A few kids chase one another around the bus. Others are playing a game of hopscotch on the dusty gravel drive.

"Hiya, Mr. Blake," says a young girl, no older than eight. She gives Vernon a wave as he climbs out of his truck. Her blond hair is pulled back in a ponytail, and she wears a brightly colored floral dress.

"Morning, Gretchen darling," Vernon replies. "What's that bus here for?"

"We're going on a field trip," Gretchen says. She twirls back and forth, the hem of her flowery dress dancing across her knees. "To see the animals at the zoo in Rush Valley."

"Ah, well, you have fun. Count the zebra's stripes for me, will ya?" Vernon asks.

Gretchen nods. She laughs and runs away as Vernon removes two wooden crates filled with milk bottles from the back of his truck. The glass bottles clink and clank together, making music as he carries them up the front steps of the orphanage, where the thick oak doors are propped open to let in the breeze.

Even so, it's hot inside. Large fans hang from the ceilings, but they only swirl the warm air around. Vernon is greeted by a *middle-aged woman. She has black hair and a pair of thick-rimmed glasses dangling from a chain around her neck. She shepherds more children outside.*

Vernon sets the crates on the wooden floor of the foyer. Then he takes off his cap and wipes sweat from his brow with a handkerchief. "Hello, Ms. Trapp," he says to the woman.

Ms. Hilda Trapp is the orphanage's director. She smiles politely at Vernon, but he can see exhaustion in her kind eyes. "Good morning, Vernon," she says. "I hope you're staying cool today."

"I am, thank you," Vernon says. "Been drinking my fair share of water."

"That's good. Just leave the milk with Ralph, as usual," she says. Then she claps loudly three times. This gets the attention of the rowdy children. "Come along," she says as they dash past on either side of her. They pass Vernon, and he takes joy in seeing the

_xcited smiles on their faces. Many of them have never been to the zoo before. "Everyone onto the bus. We must keep to our schedule."

And then Ms. Trapp is gone, out the door in the wake of frenzied children.

Ralph, the orphanage's head custodian, appears as Vernon hears the rumbling sound of the bus outside, setting off on its journey. Ralph's bald head glistens and his navy blue shirt is stained dark by sweat in his armpits and around his neck. He leads Vernon down a hall, into the kitchen, and finally to the walk-in refrigerator, where Vernon leaves the two crates of milk. They chat for a while — both are baseball fans and share a love for the local team — before Vernon bids him goodbye and is on his way.

There is no driver's-side door on Vernon's delivery truck. His view of the farmlands along the road from Washburn Orphanage back to Rush Valley is clear. The corn planted in rows is about three feet high now. "Knee-high by the Fourth of July," is how his daddy always puts it.

Soon he is on County Road Sixty-One. There is no other traffic. Not a single car passes him in either direction.

He is not sure how or why, but as Vernon nears the Sterling River, a sense of dread washes over him. It makes his blood run cold. Despite the brutal heat, he shivers. He can see the river ahead, thick and twisting, carving in wide arcs across the grasslands until it meets up with the mighty Mississippi River about a hundred miles to the east. Tall, narrow trees line the banks of the river.

The road rises, and Vernon presses his foot down hard on the gas pedal. His truck is old, and it takes every bit of the engine's power to make it up the hill. At the top of the incline, there's a bridge that crosses the river.

It's not until Vernon has reached the bridge that he sees the twisted, broken metal guardrail and the twin trails of curving, black tire tracks that cross the road's yellow dashed line like streaking comets. They lead to the bridge's edge, where the guardrail built to protect passing vehicles from the fifty-plus-foot drop to the water has been split in two.

It seems a large vehicle has crashed into the bridge and plummeted into the river.

"Oh my dear Lord," Vernon whispers. He stops the delivery truck and leaps out. He runs across the bridge as fast as his legs will take him.

He stops about fifteen feet from the edge of the bridge. Then he cautiously creeps forward, afraid of what he might see in the river's churning waters.

When he finally musters the courage to peer over the edge of the bridge, Vernon's heart feels like it might shatter in his chest.

The river is churning, silt and dirt stirred up by the crash making the water muddy and *unclear. But just beneath the river's surface, Vernon sees the rear emergency door of a yellow and white school bus.*

"No!" Vernon cries, but there is no one to hear him. His knees turn to rubber, and he falls to the hard, hot asphalt. After a moment his instincts kick in, and he tries to climb down the embankment, to somehow find his way to the riverbank. But it is too steep. One false move, and he too could plunge into the water. He sees no survivors, hears no cries for help.

Vernon runs to his truck and drives back to the orphanage as fast as he can, silently urging the old vehicle to move faster. When he arrives, he spies Ralph nearby, hammering a fallen piece of fencing in place.

"Quick!" Vernon shouts. "There's been a terrible accident."

He quickly tells Ralph what he has seen. Horrified, Ralph contacts the local police.

Hours pass. Vernon and Ralph stand together at the edge of the bridge, helpless, while police swarm the riverbanks. Divers with huge tanks of oxygen on their backs search underwater.

Finally, as dusk settles across the sky, Sterling's chief of police gives them the heartbreaking news.

"Sorry to have to tell you this," the chief says. He holds his hat in his hands and runs his fingers nervously along the brim. "But it appears that a tire on the bus blew out at the worst possible time. Nothing the driver could do about it. My deepest condolences."

"Did . . . did anyone make it?" Ralph asks.

The chief bites his bottom lip and then answers, "No. Afraid not."

Ralph breaks down, weeping like a child. Vernon, too stunned to speak, simply nods.

As the chief walks away, he whispers, "All those kids . . . just . . . gone."

* * *

Daniel stopped talking. The silence surrounding them was so thick, Emma could almost feel it weighing down on her shoulders.

"Whoa," Connor whispered.

Emma tried to speak, but her lips were dry. She took a sip of her soda. Her food sat forgotten in front of her. Then she asked, "How many children were on the bus?"

"Thirty-seven," Daniel said. "And five adults, including Ms. Trapp and the bus driver."

A tear streaked down Lucy's face, and Emma saw her quickly wipe it away.

Daniel finished his story. "So the legend says if you drive onto the bridge and stop your car, you can still hear their ghosts screaming."

Goose bumps washed over Emma's arms and made the hair on the back of her neck stand on end. "Have you ever tried it?" she asked.

Daniel nodded.

"And?" Emma asked.

Daniel shook his head. "Nothing yet," he said. "But these bridges? They're everywhere. Places where people . . . you know . . . fell into the water and drowned. Their spirits are still tied to the place where they died. Forever."

They sat in silence. Emma knew a lot of ghost stories. She devoured books and movies about ghosts and zombies and all things supernatural. But a ghost story — a *true* ghost story — that had supposedly happened so close to her hometown? That was something new.

"Everything all right over here?"

The waitress's voice startled Emma. Lucy, too. She jumped so high in her seat, her knee banged into the bottom of the table. The dishes rattled, and Connor had to quickly grab his cup of soda before it toppled over.

Connor laughed.

"Yes," Lucy said, embarrassed. "Everything is good."

Emma no longer cared about making their curfew. The night had become something far different from what she'd expected, an adventure waiting to be taken. Maybe it was Daniel's story, or the threat of letting a possibility slip through her fingers, or a healthy combination of both, but Emma had made a decision, and she wasn't going to back down from it.

"I want to see the orphanage," she said.

CHAPTER 5

When he heard Emma's request, Connor dropped what remained of his burger onto his plate. "Wait, what did you say, Em?"

"I want to see the orphanage," Emma repeated. "The abandoned Washburn building."

Lucy's jaw dropped, as if Emma had just suggested the most horrible thing in the world. "You can't be serious," she said, her voice shaking a bit.

"I'm totally serious," said Emma.

"For real?" Connor asked.

"For real," Emma answered.

And she meant it. Emma was no scaredy-cat. She was filled with curiosity. But she didn't know what she hoped to see at the abandoned orphanage. It wasn't like the *building* had started the whole legend.

"All right," Connor said. He smiled from ear to ear. "That's what I'm talking about. Daniel, you can get us there, right?"

"Yeah, I know the way," Daniel said.

Connor slammed a fist against the table, making their plates and cups rattle. "Then let's do this," he said.

They hurried to finish eating and paid for their meal with a handful of crumpled bills. When they were back in the car and pulling out of the parking lot, Connor was so excited, he nearly hit a green sedan driving into the lot. The driver of the car honked.

"Jeez, Connor, be careful," Lucy said. "Try not to get us killed *before* we get to our super-scary, abandoned, and probably haunted destination."

Connor chuckled and then cranked the stereo volume up.

Emma felt a cold hand slide on top of hers, and she looked over at Daniel.

"Are you sure you want to do this?" he asked. There seemed to be genuine concern in his eyes.

She smiled. "It's just a silly old building, right?"

"I suppose," he said.

They drove out past the edge of town, onto the two-lane highway that wove between Sterling and Rush Valley. It was another ten minutes or so before Daniel pointed and said, "There. See that windmill?"

"Barely," Connor said. He flicked on the car's high beams, revealing a bent windmill and a cluster of evergreen trees ahead on their right. A gravel road ran beside them.

"Take a right," Daniel directed.

Connor did.

Aside from the faint blue glow of the moon above, the road and surrounding farmland was pitch black. The car's headlights cut through the darkness. Even on the back roads, Connor drove fast.

It's like he thinks the Washburn building is going to disappear before we get there, Emma thought.

When she saw the building in the hazy distance, Emma's breath caught in her throat. It was mostly cloaked in shadow, but the building's silhouette alone was enough to make her heart beat a little faster and her blood race a little quicker.

The driveway leading to the orphanage was now only a pair of tire ruts in the gravel. It seemed as if a few cars had been there recently, matting down the shrubs and weeds that grew across the road.

Probably teenagers out partying, Emma thought. *I hope no one's here right now.*

They were in luck — no cars were parked at the orphanage. The place was empty.

Connor drove the car slowly up the hard-packed dirt road, stopping in front of the building. He parked the car, leaned back in his seat, and let out a deep breath.

They were silent for a moment. The car's radio was still turned low, and the music coming from the speakers was nothing more than mumbling noise.

"You guys still want to do this?" Connor asked as he craned his neck to look up at the building.

"Sure," Daniel said quietly.

Emma bit her lip as she thought about it. *You're not a coward if you change your mind,* she told herself.

"Em?" Connor had his hand on the door handle, already opening it.

"Yeah," she said.

"You guys are ridiculous," Lucy said under her breath.

Emma climbed out of the car's backseat. She could feel her whole body shaking in small tremors, but it wasn't from the cold.

There's something strange in the air, Emma thought, as the three of them stood outside the car. It took her a moment to realize what it was: it was so quiet. There were no crickets chirping or bugs humming in the weeds. On a fall night like this, the insects were usually a symphony of sound, buzzing so loud it could drive you crazy.

But around the Washburn building, it was dead silent.

From inside the car, Emma heard a soft *thunk.* Lucy had locked the doors. Her face appeared in the driver's-side window. "I love you all," she said, her voice muffled by the glass, "but I'm not crazy. Please don't die."

"Open the trunk," Connor said as he and Daniel walked around to the back of the car.

Lucy did. Then she rolled down the window and beckoned Emma over. "Are you sure you guys should go?" she asked. "Isn't it kind of dangerous?"

"Luce, I'm sure it'll be fine," Emma replied. "Stop worrying."

Lucy sighed, rolling her window back up.

Emma looked over at the building. From what she could see in the moonlight, the abandoned two-story structure was made of deep-red brick. It was crumbling in places. Large chunks of stone lay in the grass near its foundation. There were several windows, many of which were broken or boarded up with slats of dirty plywood. One wall was overgrown with tangled, clawing ivy.

Connor lifted the trunk open. It was filled with junk, everything from shower curtains to a toaster to a power drill. Connor liked to brag that he had anything and everything you could ever possibly need in his car's trunk. "One of us has to be prepared when the zombie apocalypse strikes," he'd often remarked when his friends teased him.

How exactly would a toaster help against the undead? Emma wondered.

Connor rooted around in the trunk for a minute. He pushed some junk aside and unzipped a duffel bag, pulling out two heavy-duty flashlights.

"Sorry, Em, I only have two," he said, passing one to Daniel and slamming the trunk shut. The noise was extremely loud in the silence.

"Why don't I get one?" Emma asked, annoyed.

Connor chuckled. "Just stay close," he said. He clicked on his flashlight. The light was weak at first, so he banged it against the palm of his hand until it shone bright.

Daniel tested his flashlight as well. Then he reached his hand out to Emma. She took it. Together, the three of them walked up to the front entrance of the Washburn building. Emma counted six wide stairs leading up to the doors. One of the wooden double doors was still closed. Someone from the city had nailed a NO TRESPASSING sign on it. The other door, however, was leaning off its busted hinges. It was like the building was inviting them to enter.

Emma took a long breath.

Daniel squeezed her hand. "Last chance," he said. "It's cool if you want to back out."

Emma shook her head. "Nope. I'm good."

Connor led the way up the steps, disappearing through the open door.

Emma cast a look back at Lucy, whose face was practically plastered against the inside of the car window, and then followed Daniel into the abandoned orphanage.

CHAPTER 6

When Emma stepped into the building, she immediately forgot why she'd even hesitated to enter. It wasn't scary at all. Sure, it was old and dusty and a little bit creepy, but there were signs of modern life everywhere. White plastic lawn chairs were arranged around a circle of large stones in the middle of the room, where the wooden floor had rotted away. *A fire pit,* she thought.

The inside of the fire pit was charred black, and though it had most likely been weeks since the last bonfire, the room still smelled faintly of burnt wood and ashes.

A metal garbage can was filled with trash, and there was even more litter strewn about the dusty wooden floor. Still, it seemed like no one had set foot in the building in years.

Above them, a shattered skylight let in a thin shaft of moonlight. On the far wall, the patterned wallpaper had been peeled entirely off, leaving sections of exposed plaster and many thin strips of wood. Colorful graffiti designs were tagged across the plaster wall, as well as numerous names and dates, like the wall was a guestbook signed by visitors. Emma walked over to study the designs.

"Check it out," Emma said, leaning toward the wall to look closer. The two boys walked across the wooden floor, their footsteps creaking and moaning, like they were stepping on the house's spine, cracking it as they went.

"Man, how big *is* this place?" Connor asked. There were two large hallways, one on either side of the foyer. He stepped over to explore the hall on the east side, shining his flashlight into the shadows.

A high-pitched hiss and snarl suddenly erupted down the hall, and in the beam of his flashlight, Connor caught a pair of glowing eyes. The creature leaped down from its perch on a windowsill and scurried toward them.

"Ahhh!" Connor stumbled backward, falling to the hardwood floor. His flashlight skittered away from him, casting the oncoming creature once again in darkness. Emma's pulse quickened. She heard the creature's claws scraping against the wood floor as it darted toward them.

Daniel grabbed her arm with one hand and pointed his flashlight down the hall at the approaching threat. "It's only a raccoon," he said as the large critter froze. He stepped toward it and shouted, "Go on! Shoo!"

The raccoon quickly scampered out of sight.

Connor jumped to his feet. "A raccoon," he said. "I knew it. Just a stupid raccoon." He brushed dust from his jeans and then scooped his flashlight off the ground.

As Daniel, Connor, and Emma continued their tour of the building's main floor, Emma began to think about how many children had lived in this building over the years. How it was a place of joy and heartbreak all at once. She pictured Daniel's great-grandfather walking through the same doors they had come in, carrying crates of cold milk.

Connor, showing off in the wake of his humiliating experience with the raccoon, explored ahead of Emma and Daniel. He ventured ahead by himself, but never so far that he was out of earshot. Emma could still see his flashlight beam and could hear him commenting on his surroundings.

Emma felt her phone vibrate — two quick bursts. A text message.

She dug the phone out of her back pocket. Sure enough, Lucy had sent her a text.

R u dead?

Emma shook her head and quietly laughed. She typed, *Yes. Emma's ghost is coming for you. BOO!*

"Is that Lucy?" Daniel asked.

"You bet," said Emma.

"I bet she's freaking out," Daniel said, "sitting in that car all alone."

"Hey, it was her choice. She could be in here with us, scaring off raccoons," Emma replied. "That was very brave, by the way."

Daniel bowed his head. "Why, thank you."

Emma's phone buzzed again — another text. *So not funny!!!!!!!!!!* Lucy wrote.

She showed the message to Daniel. "Ten exclamation points. Lucy means business."

Sorry, Emma typed. *We're fine.* Then she slid the phone back into her pocket.

The rest of the rooms down the hall were practically empty . . . except for cobwebs and dirt. Many of them looked like they might have been offices. A warped wooden desk still sat in the middle of one. In another, a pair of metal filing cabinets lay toppled over on the floor.

The west hall led to a spacious dining room. An ancient chandelier hung from the ceiling, wrapped in a cocoon of spiderwebs. Dead, dried insects were woven in the webs, trapped forever.

Beside the dining hall was the kitchen. It had a cracked tile floor, cabinets with no doors, and an industrial-size ceramic sink. A large metal door led to what was once a walk-in refrigerator and freezer. Chains were wrapped around its handles with a giant padlock that kept them in place.

Emma put her hand on the metal door. It was cool to the touch. "Can you imagine?" she asked Daniel quietly. "Your great-grandpa used to visit here all the time. That's pretty amazing."

Daniel smiled. "Yeah. Yeah, it is," he replied.

"Guys," Connor said. He ducked behind the far wall, into a small alcove. Then he poked his head back out. "There's a set of stairs leading to the second floor."

"Cool," Emma said. She and Daniel followed Connor up the winding wooden staircase, which creaked and shuddered with each footstep.

At the top of the stairs were more hallways branching off in different directions. One led to what looked like bathrooms. Another led to a room whose walls were lined with empty, broken shelves. *Probably a library,* Emma thought.

Down the third hallway, though, was a series of doors that all led to the same room.

"Whoa," Emma said as they walked through one of the doors.

The room was long, stretching the length of the building's second story, and it featured a sloped ceiling and a wall lined with windows. Many were broken, shuttered up with planks of weathered plywood like the ones Emma had seen outside. Under the windows was a row of small beds. Some still had mattresses, tattered and torn with their coils bursting out. Many had only the skeletal wooden frames. A few were turned on their sides — probably from past explorers.

"This must be where the kids slept," Emma whispered.

"All in one room?" Connor asked. He whipped his flashlight back and forth. What he was searching for, Emma had no idea.

But it seemed that the bedroom was not exciting enough for him. "I'm gonna keep looking," he said, disappearing down the hall.

Suddenly, the temperature seemed to plummet. Emma shivered and wrapped her arms around herself. *It's probably just the broken windows letting in drafts of cold air,* Emma told herself.

She turned to Daniel and asked, "So, did your great-grandpa ever tell you exactly why they shut this place down? I mean, I can assume, but . . ."

Daniel shook his head. "He only told me that Ms. Trapp was the orphanage's compass, always pointing to true north. When she and the kids . . . well, when the bus went off the bridge, the river swallowed Washburn's heart and soul. The county shuttered the doors shortly after and relocated the rest of the orphans."

"So there were some kids who weren't on the field trip?" Emma asked.

"I think there were a few kids who were sick, and a couple who stayed back because they were being punished," Daniel said. "They were doing chores around the building instead —"

"Hey, Daniel!" Connor's voice echoed down from the hall, startling Daniel and Emma. They quickly ran back to the hallway.

"What is it?" Daniel yelled back. "Are you okay?"

"Yeah! Gimme a hand! This door is stuck!"

Emma nodded toward Connor's voice. "Go," she said. "Help him out. I want to check out the bedroom some more."

"You'll be okay by yourself? What about the flashlight?" Daniel asked, holding it up.

Suddenly, Emma was struck by an idea. *Why didn't I think of it before?* she asked herself.

She dug her cell phone out of her pocket again. Then she turned on the flashlight app, which cast a whitish light in front of her. "You guys are so old school," she said with a smile.

Daniel smiled back and then disappeared down the corridor, taking the majority of the light with him.

Emma held her phone out in front of her as she walked back through the doorway. The light cast shadows that danced off the wall. She could still make out the bed frames, though, and she walked closer to inspect them. Some had scratches in the wood, initials or designs carved into them. The letters and drawings looked like they'd been put there by children. There was a heart on one bed, a smiley face on another.

As Emma crouched beside one of the beds, a glint of something metal on the floor caught the light. It was under the bed frame, in a pile of rubble. Chunks of brick.

Stones. Broken glass. Layers of dust. Emma dropped to her knees, reached under the bed, and plucked the item out of the pile.

"What in the world?" she whispered.

She stood up, holding the item out and shining the light on it.

It was a small necklace — probably made for a child. Its thin chain was kinked from years of lying forgotten in the debris. There was a teardrop-shaped charm on it, the size of a pebble.

Emma tried to see if it would open, if maybe it was a locket that contained an old photograph of its owner. But no. It was just a charm. She slid it between her fingers, wiping the dust and grime away with her thumb.

The light from Emma's phone flickered, as if it was about to turn off. *Weird,* she thought. *My battery shouldn't even be close to dead.*

As the light faded, Emma decided she needed to find the boys. She needed the light they both had, but she also wanted to see if they'd found anything else of interest.

"Guys!" she hollered. "You've got to see this necklace I found."

BANG!

Somewhere nearby, a door slammed shut. The noise echoed through the hall and into the bedroom, making Emma's heart nearly crash through her ribcage.

And then, with one last flicker, her phone screen went black. She gasped and shook the phone, as if the movement would spark it back to life.

It didn't work.

Emma's phone was dead, leaving her in the darkness.

Alone.

CHAPTER 7

"Daniel?" Emma stood rooted in place. She didn't want to panic and run and then trip over something and twist her ankle. So she let her eyes adjust to the new darkness before moving.

"Connor?" she called.

There was still some moonlight coming in through cracks around the boarded-up windows. One window on the far end of the room was still intact, but its glass was fogged and hard to see through.

"Guys! Where did you go? I need some light over here!" she shouted.

She strained to hear them. Nothing. There was a soft thunking sound coming from somewhere in the building. Footsteps, maybe?

Frustrated, she clutched the necklace in her hand. *Looks like I'm going to have to stumble out of here,* she thought. *Awesome.*

Suddenly the necklace in her hand burned very cold. Frigid. It felt like she was gripping dry ice.

"Ah!" Emma cried in pain. She instinctively dropped the necklace to the floor, and it landed at her feet. She shook her hand and wiggled her fingers. "Whoa. What was *that* all about?"

Emma scanned the far wall for the nearest door. She was ready to get out of this place, head back to the car, and sit with Lucy until the guys arrived and they could go home.

As she was about to take her first step, Emma stopped. Though she'd only just found it, and it was a cheap trinket whose owner was long gone, she suddenly couldn't bear the thought of leaving the necklace behind. She imagined it lost among the debris until either time or a bulldozer brought the building down. The necklace was once someone's possession. It had been loved, cherished. She couldn't leave without it.

Emma toed the floor in front of her until she heard the scrape of metal against wood. She bent down, carefully touching the necklace to see if it was still cold.

It wasn't.

She scooped it up, slid it onto her wrist, and wrapped the chain around her fingers twice. She held the teardrop charm in her palm and squeezed her hand closed. Then she held the other arm in front of her to avoid ramming her nose into a wall or something, and started to walk.

She walked out of the bedroom to the hallway, where there was a little more light — enough to make her way safely to the stairs.

The boys must be down another hallway, she thought. *The wind must have slammed the door closed behind them.*

Emma didn't remember it being windy outside, though. *And how exactly would a door in the middle of the building's second floor catch enough of a breeze to slam it closed?* she wondered.

But soon she decided that she was overthinking it. Connor had probably slammed the door shut on purpose to try to frighten her.

Like the time her brother Peter had strung one of their dad's hats on the end of a fishing line and then dangled the pole outside of her bedroom window while she, Lucy, and a couple of their friends were having a sleepover and watching television at one in the morning.

"What is that? A ghost?" Lucy had shrieked when she'd seen the hat floating in thin air. She and their other friends had screamed and slid into a huddle.

Emma had known better. She'd walked right out of her room, through the dining room, and out onto the back deck, where she'd found Peter holding the fishing pole.

They both had laughed hysterically. Then she'd shoved him and said, "Idiot."

Thinking of Peter helped Emma stay calm. She reached the staircase and placed a hand on each of the nearby walls. Emma kept her right fist closed around the necklace and walked carefully down the steps.

Before she knew it, she was back in the kitchen. There were no lights or windows. It was pitch black and silent. So silent she could hear each breath she took.

And then there was laughing.

It *sounded* like laughter, at least. But not Connor's boisterous laugh — the one that always made him double over, out of breath. This was a lilting sound, like wind chimes in the breeze. Almost like a little kid. But it couldn't be . . . could it?

"Stop it, Emma," she told herself. Even at a whisper, it sounded like a shout. "You're hearing things. Just keep moving."

So she did, shuffling slowly, her hands stretched out in front of her. She felt the cool metal of the door to the walk-in fridge and then the porcelain sink. Twenty steps more, and she felt the wooden doorframe. As she stepped through, she could sense the openness of the dining hall in front of her.

The rest of the way out of the building was fairly easy. The dining hall was spacious enough that Emma didn't have to worry about tripping over anything. Once she was in the foyer, the broken skylight and unhinged door offered enough light to guide her out.

Strange. I kind of expected the guys to be waiting for me here, Emma thought when she realized the foyer was empty.

As she slid past the front door and out onto the stairs, she saw Lucy still locked in the car, her face lit by the glow of her phone screen. When Lucy turned and saw Emma bounding down the stairs, she sat up so quickly, the phone flew from her hands.

Emma headed toward the passenger side of the car. As she did, she slid the necklace off her hand and into the front pocket of her jeans. She wasn't sure exactly why, but she didn't want Lucy to see the trinket.

Lucy rolled down the window. "Oh my gosh. You're okay," she said, like she really thought Emma was going to get swallowed by the building and never return.

"Have you seen the guys?" Emma asked.

Lucy shook her head.

"Huh." Emma turned away from the car and peeked around one side of the building. She looked for glimpses of light in the shadowy, broken windows.

Nothing.

It was almost like the guys had just . . . *disappeared.*

Well, that's dumb, she told herself. *Of course they didn't disappear.*

Emma considered going back inside to look for them. She checked her phone once more, saw that it was still dead, and changed her mind.

Instead, she climbed the front steps again and poked her head through the doorway. "Daniel!" she shouted. "Connor!"

Her words echoed in the foyer. A bird or bat or something flapped its wings and swooped down from the ceiling and out into the night sky.

Emma stood on the top step, just outside the building. She turned toward the car again and saw Lucy looking up at her in anticipation.

Emma shrugged. "Nothing."

Lucy's eyes grew wide as saucers. She pointed at Emma, stabbing her finger against the closed window. She was trying to say something, but her words were muffled behind the glass.

"What?" Emma asked, confused.

Lucy kept pointing as she rolled down the window. "Behind you!" she shouted.

Emma turned her head quickly to see a giant shadow looming in the doorway, and two arms reached out to grab her.

CHAPTER 8

The shadowy figure lunged toward Emma. Startled, she threw her arms up to protect herself.

"Boo!" Connor clicked on his flashlight and pointed the beam under his chin, shrouding his face in deep, menacing shadows. He wiggled his eyebrows and smiled. "Did I scare you?"

Emma elbowed him hard in the stomach. He coughed. "Did you not hear me?" she asked. "I was calling out for you guys."

Connor scrunched up his face and massaged his stomach. "Ow," he said.

"You're strong." He shook his head. "Didn't hear you. Sorry."

"Where's Daniel?" Emma asked.

"Here," Daniel said, appearing in the doorway behind Connor.

"What happened to you guys?"

"We found another set of steps leading all the way down to the cellar," Connor explained. "It was so awesome. Super cold down there, though."

For just a moment, Emma was envious.

"There wasn't anything *that* impressive," Daniel said. "Just an old storage space with some furniture and a pantry with a few jars on the shelves."

"I dared Daniel to crack one open and eat a pickled egg. He said no," Connor said.

"Can we get out of here?" Lucy called from the car. "I've had my fair share of heebies *and* jeebies for one night."

"Then you're not gonna love where we're heading next, Luce," Connor said with a sly smile, walking toward the car. He opened the driver's-side door and slid behind the wheel.

"Wait, what? What do you mean?" Lucy's tone was a mixture of fear and anger.

"We're not coming all this way without seeing that bridge," Connor said.

"Seeing *what*?" she shrieked.

Emma, too, was starting to feel anxious, though she couldn't explain why. She walked over to the car and threw open the door to the backseat. As she was about to climb in, a blast of cold wind whipped through the trees, making the branches sway. The sound they made as the gust sliced through them and pulled their leaves free was almost like screaming. In her pocket, the necklace seemed to freeze again, so much so that she could feel it through her jeans.

"You okay, Emma?" Daniel asked. He placed a hand on her shoulder.

She nodded. "Yep," she said. "Just excited to see the bridge."

Then she gave one last look at the run-down Washburn building before climbing into the car.

They drove along gravel roads, past farmhouses both occupied and abandoned, past fields of corn and beans almost ready to harvest, and past barren rows of tilled, dry soil where crops had already been collected.

Lucy fought hard for Connor to turn around, to go back the way they came. "I'm tired," she said. "Let's do this another night." When that wasn't enough, she began demanding. "Connor, stop the car *now*," she said. "Unless you want to be single again."

It was an empty threat, though, and Emma knew it. Lucy was head over heels for Connor, and she would never break up with him over this.

Connor knew it, too. "Come on," he said. "Where's your sense of adventure?"

"I'm dating *you*, aren't I?" Lucy grumbled. "That's enough of an adventure for me."

Emma and Daniel sat in the backseat and said nothing. Daniel nervously fiddled with the flashlight in his hands.

Emma was amazed at how many back roads there were in the area. She'd lived in Sterling her whole life and had spent a good portion of her childhood visiting Lucy's grandpa's farm just outside of town. But she'd never realized how many roads were out here among the farmland.

Daniel directed Connor from the backseat. They didn't have to travel far. After only a handful of turns and a long stretch of lonely gravel, Daniel finally said, "It's just up ahead, on the right."

Connor cranked the wheel and brought the car to a stop. Glowing bright orange in the glare of the headlights was an old gate blocking the road. A sign fastened to the gate read NO TRESPASSING and listed how much violators could be fined for breaking the law.

"Come on, Daniel, help me out," Connor said as he got out of the car, leaving his door hanging wide open. Daniel followed. Together, the two teens lifted the huge gate and swung it around so that it was no longer blocking the road.

"I've got a really bad feeling about this, Em," Lucy said under her breath.

Emma leaned forward and gave her friend's shoulder a squeeze. "It's gonna be okay, Luce. It's just a bridge."

"A *haunted* bridge," replied Lucy.

"Point taken," Emma said. *It is kind of creepy, I guess,* she admitted to herself.

Connor wiped his hands on his pants, smudging them with dirt. Then he gave the girls a double thumbs-up before he and Daniel rejoined them.

"And away we go," Connor said, putting the car in gear and driving past the gate.

The gravel road continued straight for a bit and then began to wind and twist. Emma tried to imagine Daniel's great-grandpa Vernon driving his delivery truck down this very road over a half-century ago. She thought about that fateful day, how he'd taken this route like he'd done hundreds of times before. How he'd been happy, oblivious to the way the world was about to change in the span of a heartbeat. How he was helpless to stop it.

As the car began to climb a hill, Emma's stomach flipped. She knew the bridge was near. Sure enough, when they reached the top and the road began to flatten, Emma saw it. The bridge was narrower than she'd imagined. The concrete was riddled with cracks and overgrown with weeds and grass. The barriers on either side were only a few feet high.

Connor slowed the car a bit as they reached the start of the bridge. Emma squeezed Daniel's hand and saw Lucy clutch the handle above her door tight enough to make her knuckles turn white.

"So, you said you've done this before?" Emma quietly asked, turning to Daniel.

He nodded.

"And nothing's happened?"

"Nope," he replied.

It wasn't the ghost story that made her nervous, though. It was the bridge itself — whether it was structurally sound enough to handle the weight of Connor's car.

At least that's what Emma kept telling herself.

CHAPTER 9

Connor drove onto the bridge and rolled his window down.

"What are you doing?" Lucy asked sharply. "Roll that up. It's freezing outside."

"How are we supposed to hear any ghosts screaming if the windows are up?" Connor asked. He leaned his head out the window. "Let's hear it, ghosties!" he shouted. "Can I get a 'whoop-whoop'?"

Nothing.

Lucy smacked him on the chest. "Knock it off, Connor," she said. "You're asking for it." Then she pulled her legs up onto the seat and wrapped her arms around them for warmth.

Emma leaned close to her window, examining the bridge's railing to see if she could figure out where the bus had gone over the edge. She didn't realize that she had pulled the necklace out of her pocket until she had the chain twirled tightly around her fingers and was squeezing the locket in her palm like it was a good-luck charm.

Connor drove down the middle of the closed bridge, his old car straddling the faded yellow dashes. When they were near the center, he brought the car to a complete stop. Then he turned the engine off and said, "So . . . uh, now what?"

Daniel shrugged his shoulders. "We wait."

And so they did. It was pure silence, except for the occasional shuffling of their bodies. Once in a while, the wind would pick up a bit, slicing through Connor's open window.

But there were no sounds coming from the bridge. No screams.

Nothing supernatural at all.

Finally, Connor said, annoyed, "Well, this was a bust." He opened his car door, turning on the dome light above them. Emma was so used to the dark that the relatively dim bulb was almost blinding.

"What are you doing?" Lucy asked.

"Just looking around," he said. "Obviously nothing is going to happen."

Connor got out of the car and took a few steps toward the edge of the bridge. After a moment, Daniel followed him.

Emma decided to join them. "Come on, Luce," she said, pulling her door handle.

Lucy sighed. "Oh, all right," she said.

The two girls stepped out of the car onto the cracked bridge. Lucy, though she was acting braver than she had all night, still scurried over and locked her arms around Connor.

"It's actually pretty peaceful out here," Daniel said. "You can see so many stars."

Emma had been so focused on the bridge and the water below that she hadn't looked up. When she did, she was amazed. The cloudless sky was splattered with a billion flickering stars. It was almost overwhelming. It made her, her friends, her life, and this silly outing seem tiny and unimportant.

"Pretty sure this is where the bus went over." Daniel's calm voice broke Emma from her temporary spell. She walked over to the guardrail, where Daniel stood examining the metal. The rail was up to Emma's waist.

No wonder the bus went over so easily, she thought. *Any vehicle could topple right off with such a small barrier.*

Sure enough, the metal near Daniel was a shade darker than the rest, and newer.

This must be where it was replaced, Emma thought.

Daniel slid his hand along the rail until he found the spot where the pieces had been welded together. The newer part of the guardrail was roughly twenty feet long.

"I dare you to look over the edge, Emma," Connor said. He was smiling at her mischievously.

She shrugged. "Okay."

Emma moved closer to the guardrail. She could hear the soft roar of the river far below. Though it had been a hot, dry summer, the current was strong, and Emma listened to the water crash against the rocks as it flowed downriver.

She craned her neck, trying to peer below, but the river was black as ink and hard to spot. She found that she was gripping the necklace so tight in her hand that she was cutting off circulation to her fingers.

A gust of wind suddenly slid up from the river and sent a chill down Emma's spine. She gasped. Then the wind howled, and in it, Emma could swear that she heard faint, high-pitched . . .

Screaming.

She staggered back a step. "I'm kinda cold," she said, not wanting to admit how scared she felt. "Luce, you wanna wait in the car with me?"

"Sure," Lucy said as she let go of Connor and latched onto Emma's arm instead. She reached down to hold Emma's hand, but instead she found a balled-up fist with a necklace wrapped around it.

"What's that?" Lucy asked.

"Nothing," Emma said. She didn't know why she felt possessive of the necklace, but she didn't like that Lucy had noticed it.

"Come on," Connor said, walking up to them. "This was a bust. Let's bail."

They all piled back into the car, Lucy taking her place beside Connor up front, Emma and Daniel in the backseat together again. Emma closed her eyes and squeezed the necklace.

Connor turned the key in the ignition.

The car didn't start.

"Weird," he said.

He tried it again. Nothing.

"What's going on?" Lucy asked. "Connor, please don't say your stupid car is dead again."

"No, it can't be. I just replaced the battery last month. It's not turning over," Connor said, scratching his head. He tried twisting the key in the ignition a third time, but the car's engine refused to even make a sound.

There was silence for a moment as they all thought about what to do next.

Thunk!

Suddenly, all four doors simultaneously locked, making Emma jump and Lucy yelp. "Connor, knock it off!" she shouted. "That's not funny."

"I . . . I didn't do it." Connor's words were laced with a hint of panic. "I swear."

Emma reached over and tried to manually unlock her door. It wouldn't budge. In front of her, Connor's open window began to slide closed. Connor threw his hands in the air. "See? I'm not doing anything!"

"Then what's going on?" Lucy asked anxiously.

Emma knew, though. She could feel the necklace in her hand turning cold. She knew then that the faint screaming sounds she'd heard while she stood at the bridge's guardrail were real.

She knew the legend was true.

All of a sudden, the car lurched, beginning to move. Not forward, though. It was skidding sideways, inch by terrifying inch, toward the guardrail. Toward the exact spot where the bus from the Washburn Orphanage had plummeted over the side.

"We're moving!" Lucy screamed. "We're moving!"

Connor tried the ignition again and again, but nothing happened. He slammed his fists against the steering wheel in frustration. "I don't know what to do!" he shouted.

Lucy was in hysterics. She hit Connor on the arm repeatedly. "I knew this was a stupid idea!"

Daniel rose up onto his knees on the seat. He braced himself and then drove his elbow hard into the window. The glass held. Again. Again.

Not even a crack.

Emma looked out her window again. Their car was now feet from the edge of the bridge. She placed her hands on the glass.

The necklace was still in her fist, clinking gently against the window. Wind slammed into the car, rocking it from side to side. She could not see the ghosts, but she could certainly feel them.

Then Lucy asked a horrifying question. "Is . . . is that water?"

Emma swung her head around to see Lucy, still crouched on her seat, pointing to the car's floor, where brown, muddied water gurgled and pooled.

"But that's impossible!" Connor shouted. He reached over and pulled Lucy onto his lap.

Emma looked down at her feet. Sure enough, water was seeping through the cracks in the doorframe and starting to cover her red sneakers. She lifted her feet out of the rising sludge.

This can't be happening, she thought. *There's no such thing as ghosts.*

Like never before, the fearless Emma Donovan felt truly terrified.

The car reached the guardrail and clanged against it. Emma heard the terrible screech of metal on metal. She pounded her fists against the glass. "Knock it off!" she shouted. Her whole body trembled with fear.

I don't want to die. I don't want to die, she thought.

"Please!" she cried. Her eyes began to water until tears streaked down her cheeks. "Please stop!"

And it did.

The car, mere inches from the bridge's edge, suddenly stopped moving.

"What's going on?" Lucy asked. She had her arm wrapped tightly around Connor's neck. "Is it over?"

Daniel stopped slamming his elbow into the window.

"I . . . I don't know," Emma answered.

Connor reached around Lucy and tried to start the car again. "Nothing," he whispered.

As if on cue, the car began to rock back and forth again. Lucy screamed at the top of her lungs. The water at Emma's feet was halfway up the seat, and it seemed to be rising faster than before.

The car lurched forward this time, skidding across the cement. Though they were still inches from the edge, it appeared as if the car was no longer destined for the river.

It was moving toward the far side of the bridge and the safety of land.

The water bubbled and swirled around. It rose above the seat, sloshing over the leather and soaking Emma's jeans. With Daniel's help, she scrambled up and crouched on the seat.

"We're going to drown!" Lucy yelled. She was clawing at Connor. Because of the steering wheel, Connor couldn't move his legs out of the water. Instead, he kept Lucy as safe and dry as he could. Daniel was throwing his whole shoulder against the window now, but it was useless. The four teens were trapped in a water-filled car.

When it reached the other side of the bridge, where the cement turned to gravel once again, the car stopped.

The necklace was ice-cold, numbing Emma's hand. Still, she plunged her hand into the water, searching madly for the door handle. She felt around until she was able to grab it, then pulled on the handle with all her strength, not expecting it to budge.

Like a miracle, though, the door swung open.

Water poured out of the car and onto the gravel road. Emma tumbled out of the open door, landing hard on her hands. It wasn't until she looked down at her palms and saw the scrapes and blood and rocks that she realized she no longer held the necklace in her fist.

It must have fallen off when I grabbed the door handle, she thought.

Right now, though, Emma didn't care. She was safe, and she had to make sure her friends were also. She staggered to her feet, turning back to the car. Daniel was climbing across the seat toward the open door.

"Come on!" Emma yelled as she reached out for him. The wind swelled at her back, slamming the car door shut before Daniel could escape. "No!" Emma shouted. She tried the door, but it was locked again. She banged on the window and saw Daniel inside doing the same. She tried the other doors, shouting, "Let them out! Please let them out!"

But the car doors remained shut, and inside, the water was rising again.

Emma repeatedly tried to open the doors, but none would budge. The water inside the car had reached the top of the windows now, and it sloshed against the glass. Emma tried to see her friends through the brown water, but all she could see were floating bits of debris swirling about. She pressed closer to the glass, straining to see inside.

Out of nowhere, the pale face of a little girl appeared in the murky water on the other side of the window.

Emma screamed and fell backward, landing hard on the gravel.

The girl in the window looked about eight years old. Her skin was nearly translucent, and the smile on her face was just a little too wide. Her blond ponytail floated and snaked behind her in the water. She wore a tattered, floral-patterned dress. And around her neck was the teardrop-shaped necklace.

The girl cocked her head to the side, staring at Emma with blank eyes.

"Lucy . . . Connor . . . Daniel . . ." Emma chanted her friends' names, praying that they would hear her, that they were somehow safe.

She got to her feet and backed up until she reached the side of the road, where the tall grass rose up to her knees. Brambles caught in the wet fabric of Emma's jeans. She couldn't take her eyes off the little girl inside the car.

Another face joined the girl — a small boy. Then another child. And another.

The car seemed to be filled with them. They pressed their small hands against the windows, their white fingers spread wide. The wind around Emma howled and screamed louder than ever before.

Afraid that she would soon suffer the same fate as her friends, that the spirits on the bridge would take her, too, Emma turned and ran off, away from the car and the gravel road and her lost friends, into the open field of rocks and grass.

She did not look back.

CHAPTER 10

Branches and weeds tore at Emma's legs as she stumbled through the grassy field over clumps of dirt, nearly falling a dozen times. And with each staggering step, she saw the children in the car.

The little girl looking out at her with blank eyes. Smiling.

Wearing the necklace.

Is that why she let me go? Emma asked herself. *Is it because I brought the necklace back to her?*

Ahead of her, the grassy landscape rose and fell. Emma's muscles burned as she climbed the first hill. Not once did she turn to look behind her. She could still hear the wind screaming. Whether it was calling out to her or whether it was simply an echo in her mind, she didn't know. She didn't *want* to know.

Emma ran, finding her way by the moonlight, until her lungs burned. When she finally stopped, she doubled over, hands on her knees, gasping for air.

Long minutes passed.

Emma stood shaking, not sure if she could continue. She had no idea where she was anymore. She couldn't see any roads or trails or the river. She was lost in the darkness.

Where is the road? she wondered. *Oh no. I . . . I should have stayed on the road, and now I'm lost . . . and where are my friends?*

The tears came easily then in loud, choking sobs. She fell to her knees in the dirt.

Emma sat on the ground and pulled her legs up to her chest. Her feet were cold, but strangely, her sneakers were no longer wet. Her jeans were torn and smeared with dirt and blood from her scraped-up palms.

I can't stay here all night, she thought as she shivered from the cold breeze. *I have to keep moving.*

She got to her feet and turned in circles, searching for any sign of civilization. A farm. A car. A road. She pulled her phone out of her pocket, doubting that it would somehow be charged and working.

She was right. It was still dead.

Beyond a large thicket of trees on her left, Emma spied a section of the dark night sky that seemed a little bit hazier than the rest, as if lit from the collective glow of a thousand lights.

That must be Sterling, Emma thought as she began to walk in that direction.

When Emma entered the canopy of trees, she ducked to avoid a low-hanging branch. She walked with her arms in front of her for safety. Dead leaves and twigs crunched and cracked beneath her sneakers like dried, brittle bones.

As she reached the other side of the thicket, Emma saw a flicker of light dance in the corner of her eye. She pushed aside an evergreen branch and strained to see the light's source.

Far in the distance, a set of headlights cut through the black night.

A road, she thought. *That must be a road.*

Emma felt a renewed strength wash over her. She burst out of the trees, into a ditch filled with large boulders and weeds. She climbed over the rocks quickly but cautiously, so as not to twist an ankle.

When she reached the top of the ditch, Emma stumbled out onto the road, right into the glare of oncoming headlights. She instinctively scrambled back to the shoulder of the road as the car's driver slammed on the brakes, and the vehicle swerved on the loose gravel.

The car stopped a few feet away from Emma.

Out of breath, she slowly lowered herself to the ground, exhausted. She looked up and tried to see the driver of the car, but all she could make out was the driver's silhouette as he exited the vehicle.

The car door slammed. "Emma! Oh, thank goodness, it's you!"

"Connor?" Emma whispered. She didn't believe it. It couldn't be him.

Could it?

A second door opened, followed by Lucy's voice. "Em! Are you all right?"

Lucy ran to Emma, fell to her knees in the gravel beside her, and hugged her close.

It really is Lucy, Emma thought. *She's warm, so warm . . . and dry.*

And most importantly, she was *alive*.

Emma hugged her friend fiercely. Her head was a cloud of confusion. She had so many questions. But for the moment, all she wanted to do was remain on the ground with Lucy.

Daniel jumped out of the car as well and walked over to the group. When Emma was finally ready to stand, he held his hand out, offering to help her to her feet.

"Thanks," Emma said to Daniel as he pulled her up from the ground.

"Let's go to the car," he said. "You're shaking like a leaf."

He put his arm around Emma's shoulders and walked with her to the car. She hesitated before climbing into the backseat, expecting to see the ghost of the little girl with the necklace waiting for her.

But the car was dry, like nothing had happened.

How is that possible? she wondered.

"Are you okay?" Daniel asked.

"I'm . . . I'm fine," Emma lied. Then she eased herself into the backseat.

Daniel started to get into the car next to her, but Lucy cut him off. "I'll sit with her," she said, climbing in beside Emma and taking her hand.

"Roll the windows down," Emma whispered. Claustrophobia was creeping in on her, making it hard to breathe.

"What?" Lucy asked.

"The windows," Emma repeated. "Open them. Leave them open. Please?"

From the driver's seat, Connor said, "Yeah. Sure thing, Em."

For a time, the ride back to Sterling was silent. The wind from the open windows was brisk and cold and made the two girls shiver even as they huddled together in the backseat.

Finally, Lucy asked, "Emma, what happened?"

She didn't know where to begin. She stumbled over her words. "I — I saw them . . . the ghosts. First I heard the screams . . . then we were trapped in the car . . . and then . . ." She trailed off.

"Trapped in the car?" Lucy asked, confused. "Emma, what do you mean? We were never trapped in the car."

"Yeah," Connor added. "We all got back in the car after standing on the bridge, but before I could start it up, you flipped out and ran away."

"We've been driving around looking for you," Lucy said. "I was so worried."

"So . . . none of you heard them?" Emma asked.

Did I imagine the whole thing? Is that possible? she wondered.

The others shook their heads. Connor looked quizzically at Emma in the rearview mirror. "You heard the ghosts, though? Did you *see* them?"

"Yeah . . . I think so."

"What exactly did you see?" Daniel asked. He turned in his seat and draped his arm over the headrest.

Emma shook her head.

Though she remembered each moment clearly, she did not want to discuss the little girl, the necklace, the ghosts, the flooded car, her drowning friends.

"It's okay," Lucy said, resting her head on Emma's shoulder. "It's been a long night. Let's just go home."

"Can you just take me back to my house?" Emma asked. She no longer wanted to sleep over at Lucy's. She wanted to be in the comfort of her own bed, the safety of her own house.

"Of course," Connor said.

"Are you sure?" Lucy asked. "You can totally stay at my house."

"I'm sure."

The rest of the ride was quiet. Emma insisted that Connor not pull into her driveway, in case it woke her parents. By the time Connor parked at the curb down the street from her house, the digital clock on the stereo read 2:33 a.m.

Lucy hugged Emma once more and then said, "Call me if you need anything, okay? This will all seem silly tomorrow morning."

Emma nodded. She hoped Lucy was right.

"Bye, Emma," Connor said, no longer loud and cocky.

"Good night, Connor."

Daniel said, "Sorry for tonight, Emma."

"It's not your fault. Really," she answered.

Emma climbed out of the car, careful not to slam the door. She took a few steps down the sidewalk and then turned back toward the black car. Its bright taillights gave off a fiery red glow despite the dust that covered them.

They had driven down gravel roads and kicked up dirt in their wake all night. A thick film of dust coated the black car.

And imprinted in the dust on the sides, the trunk, and the chrome fender were handprints.

Emma felt fear grip her all over again, making her chest tighten and her breath quicken.

Tiny, child-like handprints. Dozens of them.

GLOSSARY

apocalypse (uh-PAH-cuh-LIPS) — a great disaster

claustrophobia (KLAWS-truh-FOH-bee-uh) — extreme fear of being in small, enclosed spaces

condolences (kuhn-DOH-luhns-ez) — expression of sympathy, especially when someone has just died

etiquette (ET-i-kit) — rules of polite behavior that most people are aware of

foyer (FOI-ur) — an entrance hall

graffiti (gruh-FEE-tee) — drawings or words people put on places they're not supposed to, such as walls of public buildings

guardrail (GAHRD-rayl) — a metal bar along the side of a road that prevents cars from driving off

incredulous (in-KREJ-uh-luhss) — unable to believe something

instinctively (in-STINGKT-uhv-lee) — done without thinking or done in a natural way

intrigued (in-TREEGD) — very interested

objections (uhb-JEK-shuhnss) — feelings of not liking something

plummet (PLUM-it) — to fall or drop suddenly, especially from a high-up place

welded (WELD-id) — joined two pieces of metal together by heating them

DISCUSSION QUESTIONS

1. Why do you think Emma didn't want to tell her friends about the necklace? Discuss some possibilities.

2. Like Daniel, who heard the story of the screaming bridge from his great-grandpa Vernon, everyone hears stories, both scary and otherwise, from their friends and family. Is there a scary story that someone has passed on to you? Share it with the group.

3. Do you think it's true that Emma never felt scared until she was standing on the bridge, hearing children screaming? Discuss why or why not.

WRITING PROMPTS

1. In the last chapter of the book, Emma sees children's handprints all over the outside of her friend's car as it drives away. Write a different ending to the story. But make sure it's still scary!

2. Write an essay about a time when you felt frightened. What was it about the situation that scared you? How did you handle it? What might you do differently if you were in that situation again?

3. Do you think Lucy is a good friend to Emma? Write a paragraph explaining why or why not.

ABOUT THE AUTHOR

Brandon Terrell has been a lifelong fan of all things spooky, scary, and downright creepy. He is also the author of numerous children's books, including six volumes in the Tony Hawk's 900 Revolution series, several Sports Illustrated Kids graphic novels, and a You Choose chapter book featuring Batman. When not hunched over his laptop writing, Brandon enjoys watching movies (horror movies especially!), reading, baseball, and spending time with his wife and two children in Minnesota.

ABOUT THE ILLUSTRATOR

Nelson Evergreen lives on the south coast of the United Kingdom with his partner and their imaginary cat. Evergreen is a comic artist, illustrator, and general all-around doodler of whatever nonsense pops into his head. He contributes regularly to the British underground comics scene, and he is currently writing and illustrating a number of graphic novel and picture book hybrids for older children.